Heather lives in Las Vegas, Nevada with her husband Kyle and three children, Ashley, Jaden, and step-son Nico. She has always loved the magic of Christmas stories. She wrote this book based on an actual event of when her son, Jaden, did indeed find the letter Santa wrote him saved on the home computer. The best explanation she could come up with was the one you will read about in the SSSH: Secret Society of Santa's Helpers. I hope this book brings young readers and parents alike as much joy as it has brought to her own children.

Heather Mirich

SSSH: THE SECRET SOCIETY OF SANTA 'S HELPERS

AUSTIN MACAULEY PUBLISHERS™

LONDON • CAMBRIDGE • NEW YORK • SHARJAH

Ordering Information:

Quantity sales: special discounts are available on quantity purchases by corporations, associations, and others. For details, contact the publisher at the address below.

First Edition Published: 2017 (Austin Macauley Publishers™ LLC)

Mirich Heather.
SSSH: The Secret Society of Santas Helpers

ISBN 9781643783086 (Paperback)
ISBN 9781643783093 (Hardback)
ISBN 9781643783109 (E-Book)

The main category of the book — Fantasy
www.austinmacauley.com/us

Second Edition (2018)
Austin Macauley Publishers™ LLC
40 Wall Street, 28th Floor
New York, NY 10005
USA

mail-usa@austinmacauley.com
+1 (646) 5125767

I dedicate this book to my children, Jaden and Ashley
who were my inspiration in writing this story.

I would like to thank my mother who blessed me with the gift
of her story telling over the years.

I had just turned nine in August, it was the end of my summer break, and I knew I was no longer a little kid. In just a few weeks I would be a fourth grader!

I spent most of the summer playing my favorite video game —Minecraft— which was awesome! Anything my imagination could dream up, I would create. Minecraft was my world, with no rules, except of course, staying alive. My mom would remind me that in order to stay alive in Minecraft, I also need to stay alive in the real world. She would make me take breaks from my game to eat dinner with the family, brush my teeth, and of course get in the shower when needed. Although I didn't want to admit it, she always took care of me. Don't tell her, but she's a pretty cool mom— most of the time.

Now that school had started and I had less time to live in my imaginary Minecraft world. Let's face it, my real life just couldn't compete. Nothing interesting ever happens, or so I thought!

It was that time of year when the fourth grade students got to choose a project for the school science fair. For once, something in school that was actually kind of fun! In the past, my mom would type up my school reports. However, this year mom told me, "If you're old enough to play games on the computer, you're old enough to type your own reports."

One night in September, I sat down to finish typing my science report, "How to Build a Solar Oven." When I began looking through the saved documents to find mine, I found something else entirely. I saw a document called, Letter from Santa to Jaden. I clicked on it immediately! There it was, the letter Santa himself wrote to me last year. The one that thanked me for being a good boy all year; the one that thanked me for being a special kid; the one that thanked me for the milk and cookies I left him.

Dear Jaden,
Thank you for being such a good boy all year long. I've been watching
you and I know you're a special kid. Your parents love you very much.
I love visiting your house because you have the best milk and cookies!
See you next year.

Love, Santa Claus

I thought, Wait, what is this? Why would the letter Santa wrote me be saved on our home computer? My imagination started going crazy, so many thoughts flooded my mind. Are those kids at school right? Is there really no Santa Claus? If there's no Santa, then who's been leaving me presents all these years? Santa has to be real, there's got to be an explanation! But, what could it be?

Several months went by and I never told my mom what I found saved on our home computer. Actually, I hadn't really given it much thought since the night I found the letter.

12

Dear Jaden

love Santa

Once Thanksgiving had passed and the weather began to get colder, it started to feel like Christmastime. December was always a fun time for our family. We baked lots of Christmas cookies, listened to our favorite Christmas music, and of course made a list of all the things my sister, Ashley, and I wanted from Santa.

But this year it felt different. I knew in my heart Santa was real, but as Christmas was getting closer I couldn't stop thinking about the letter I had found. I needed to figure out a way to find out if Santa was real or not!

If Santa wasn't real then where did all the presents come from? I don't think my mom would buy me ALL those presents and just say they were from Santa. If she bought me a present, trust me, she would want me to know the present was from her. She ALWAYS reminded me of all the video games and toys she bought for my sister and me, and also how much money they cost. So I doubt they came from her. However, suppose they did? That would be a lot to pull off! My mom is also the most honest person I know, so I don't think she would lie to me all these years. She always knows when I'm lying, so I think I would be able to tell if she was lying.

16

The weather was starting to get cold out and my mom does NOT like the cold! That sure doesn't keep her from going out to the mall; which seems to be ALL the time! Last December she started wearing this ugly red Christmas hat. She looked ridiculous in that hat with her big curly hair, but she would say it keeps her ears warm. Did I mention we live in sunny Las Vegas? The summers are hot and the winters are actually quite cold! But most of the year, when she's not at work, she's pretty much in flip flops and tank tops and NEVER a hat. That's why I didn't understand why she started wearing that ugly red hat last year. This December she's wearing that same ugly red hat again! For Christmas I think I'm going to get her a different hat, one that's not so embarrassing!

My sister and I had an extra-long Christmas Wish List this year. I made sure of it! I knew there would be no way my mom would be able to buy most of the presents without the help of Santa. Since I don't get everything on my list, I made it a point to circle the one thing I wanted more than anything; possibly even more than learning the truth about Santa Claus! It was the Blade 360X yellow motorcycle. It was more of an electric scooter, but we all called it a motorcycle. It was COOL! The kids in the neighborhood all had one and I wanted it so much! My mom would tell me over and over how I was too young and they weren't safe. I didn't care, I just wanted one!

Christmas Eve had finally arrived and I was so excited for Christmas morning. I had been watching my mom closely to see if she bought any of the presents that were on my Christmas Wish List. I looked in all the possible hiding places, including many she didn't think I knew of. So far, she was either really sneaky or she wasn't Santa Claus.

We continued our Christmas Eve tradition of putting out a plate of our special chocolate chip cookies and milk. We knew Santa would be thirsty after all those cookies. We wrote a thank you letter to Santa and went to our bedrooms. Ashley was only six years old, and as much as she tried to stay awake, she fell asleep right away. Last year I only made it to 11:00 at night. Not this year, I knew I was going to stay up all night long! I would either see Santa with my own two eyes or catch my mom pretending to be Santa Claus!

I waited until after midnight and went downstairs. I could actually hear someone in the family room. This was it! I was going to finally find out the truth about Santa Claus . . . whether I was ready for it or not! I peeked around the corner and saw a shadow by the tree. It definitely wasn't the shadow of Jolly Old St. Nick and it didn't look like my mom's shadow either. As I got closer I noticed the shadow had huge ears, and they sure were pointy! They looked an awful lot like elf ears!

20

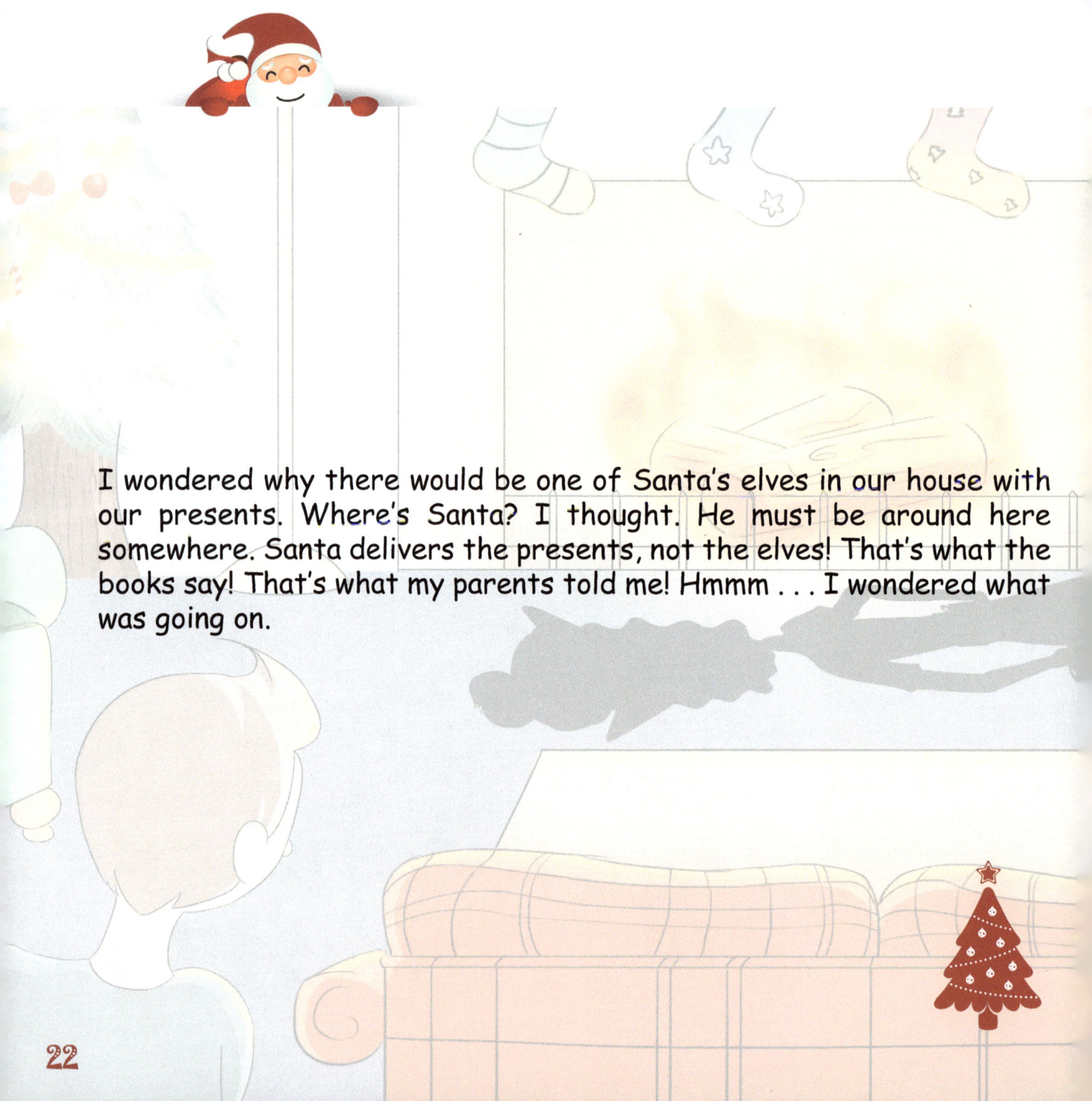

I wondered why there would be one of Santa's elves in our house with our presents. Where's Santa? I thought. He must be around here somewhere. Santa delivers the presents, not the elves! That's what the books say! That's what my parents told me! Hmmm . . . I wondered what was going on.

22

In a moment of confusion and disbelief, I ran to our front yard and then to our back yard. I didn't see a red-nose reindeer, no sleigh, no Santa Claus! The only thing I could see was our swimming pool and our overdone Christmas decorations.

23

I ran back to where the elf was and this time I caught a glimpse of the elf's face and that's when I started to faint. I didn't hit the floor though, because I was caught by . . . ummmm . . . my Mom! Or should I say my Mom who looked an awful lot like an elf! That's right friends, MY MOM WAS THE ELF! Those pointy big ears belonged to her. She must have been hiding them behind that ugly red hat!

I nervously said, "Mom, you have some major explaining to do!" My mom spent the next hour telling me how she became one of Santa's Helpers. She went on to tell me that last year was the first time she became an Elf Mom. She explained, "Not all moms are chosen to become an Elf Mom." She didn't even realize that there was such a thing until last year.

She went on, "Santa calls on Moms all over the world to find special Santa helpers, also known as Elf Moms. The North Pole elves are great at making toys and gifts for children all over the world, but sometimes Santa needs extra help to buy things that the elves can't make. Moms can help with purchases online and buy gifts from the local stores. For instance, when kids like your sister ask for designer clothes from a certain store, Santa needs us to help with those purchases too." Mom continued, "When Santa asked if I could help him out over the next couple of years, I just couldn't say no to Santa. So here I am, your mom, one of the chosen Elf Moms. Last year was my first year as an Elf Mom. I was in charge of buying some of the gifts for you and your sister and other kids too. I put your presents from Santa by the tree. I got to eat all those yummy cookies. I even typed out the thank you letter from Santa on our home computer. Santa told me what to say, but it was easier for him if I typed it out.

santa's toy shop

"Now, that was the fun part of being an Elf Mom. The part Santa left out was that my ears would grow into elf ears around Christmastime. That's why I always have that ugly red Christmas hat on. Nothing else would hide my enormous elf ears." We both started to giggle.

"Oh, I get it!" I exclaimed. "Elf Moms help Santa by buying and delivering presents!"

"Yes," mom replied. "Santa does his very best to make it to every home around the world. However, on the rare occasion he must skip a home we are his backup helpers. He knows moms do such a good job taking care of everyone that we would make perfect Santa helpers."

28

santa's toy shop

29

The Secret Society of Santa's Helpers
Est. 1982.

So it turns out Elf Moms were started way back in 1982 My grandmother, Melinda, was a first generation Elf Mom. There are so many now that they created the Secret Society of Santa's Helpers, for short they go by SSSH, as in "keep a secret". There have even been a select few dads that have been enlisted by Santa himself. Mom looked into my eyes and said, "So Jaden, now that you know, you must also keep the very special secret of SSSH because someday you may be called by Santa to be part of SSSH"

I understood now. The secret of SSSH was safe with me. I was happy to finally learn the truth. Now I know Santa is real, he just has a little extra help.

Elf Mom Melinda
(1982 - 1985)

Elf Mom Bethanne
(1982 - 1985)

Elf Mom Beverly
(1982 - 1987)

Elf Mom Marianne
(1982 - 1985)

Elf Mom Jean
(1982 - 1984)

Elf Mom Betty Ann
(1982 - 1987)

The Secret Society of Santa's Helpers
Est. 1982.

Elf Mom Melinda
(1982-1985)

Elf Mom Bethanna
(1982- 1985)

Elf Mom Beverly
(1982 – 1987)

Elf Mom Marianne
(1982 – 1985)

Elf Mom Jean
(1982 – 1984)

Elf Mom Rose Ann
(1982 –1987)

Elf Mom Marianne
(1982 – 1985)

Elf Mom Jean
(1982 – 1984)

Elf Mom Rose Ann
(198   87)

31

That night I told my mom that I thought she was a cool mom and finally thanked her for everything she does. I was also relieved to know that my mom's ears would be going back to normal on Christmas morning, and she could finally stop wearing that ugly red hat. I gave my mom a big hug and we both went to sleep. After all, it was Christmas morning in a few hours. Who knew the real world could be just as exciting as my video games. I know . . . I know . . . Mom knew, of course!

If you were wondering if Santa gave me the Blade 360X yellow motorcycle, the answer is a big NO; I got a toy model instead. Apparently, Santa got the message that my mom thinks they are unsafe. (By the way, Mom and Santa, opening a toy model motorcycle on Christmas morning wasn't that funny to me!) But I did get a new PlayStation 4 video game console, and it even came with the PlayStation 4 edition of Minecraft, which is pretty awesome! So I guess it doesn't completely stink that my mom knows Santa.

So kids, if you ever sneak out of your bedroom on Christmas Eve and see your mom carrying Christmas presents, remember your mom too could be one of the chosen Elf Moms. You just might want to go hat shopping for her next year.

The end

P.S. Wait a second, why does my dad wear that big ugly hat at Easter time? Oh boy, I have my work cut out for me. Let the next adventure begin ...

35